For my dear friend
Jo Coleman
with love

Foxy in Love
Copyright © 2013 by Emma Dodd
All rights reserved. Manufactured in China.
No part of this book may be used or reproduced in any manner whatsoever without
written permission except in the case of brief quotations embodied in critical articles
and reviews. For information address HarperCollins Children's Books, a division of
HarperCollins Publishers, 10 East 53rd Street, New York, NY 10022.
www.harpercollinschildrens.com

Library of Congress Cataloging-in-Publication Data is available.
Library of Congress catalog card number: 2012015522
ISBN 978-0-06-201422-1 (trade bdg.) — ISBN 978-0-06-201423-8 (lib. bdg.)

The artist used pen, ink, and Photoshop to create the digital illustrations for this book.
Typography by Dana Fritts
13 14 15 16 17   SCP   10 9 8 7 6 5 4 3 2 1 ❖ First Edition

EMMA DODD

Foxy in love

HARPER

An Imprint of HarperCollinsPublishers

It was almost Valentine's Day. Emily was making a special card, but she was having trouble deciding what to draw.

Just then, Foxy appeared at the window. "What are you doing?" he asked Emily.

"Hello, Foxy. I'm trying to think of all the things I love so I can draw them in my card," said Emily. "But I love everything! I don't know where to start."

Foxy was sure he could help.
"Think hard, Emily," he said.
"What do you love best of all?"

"Oh yes! I know!" said Emily.

"Of course you do," Foxy said, smiling shyly.

"I love **balloons!**" Emily said.

"Balloons!" said Foxy with a sigh. He was very disappointed, but he waved his magical tail back and forth and back and forth anyway.

"Ta-da! Balloons!"

Emily laughed. "Those are **raccoons,** not **balloons!**"

Foxy tried again, and this time he filled the room with colorful balloons.

"Oh, thank you, Foxy!" exclaimed Emily.

"You're welcome," Foxy said. "Now, can you think of something else you love?"

Emily thought for a moment.
"I love pots of **hot chocolate**—
with **marshmallows!**"

Foxy wasn't sure he heard her correctly. But he swished his tail, and suddenly there was a . . .

. . . bathtub full of **hot chocolate** and **marshmallows!**
"That's lots of hot chocolate!" she said. "I just wanted a pot!
Never mind, Foxy. I thought of something else."
"You did?" asked Foxy hopefully.

"I love **flowers!**" Emily said.
"Flowers?" Foxy sighed again and waved his tail. "Coming right up!"

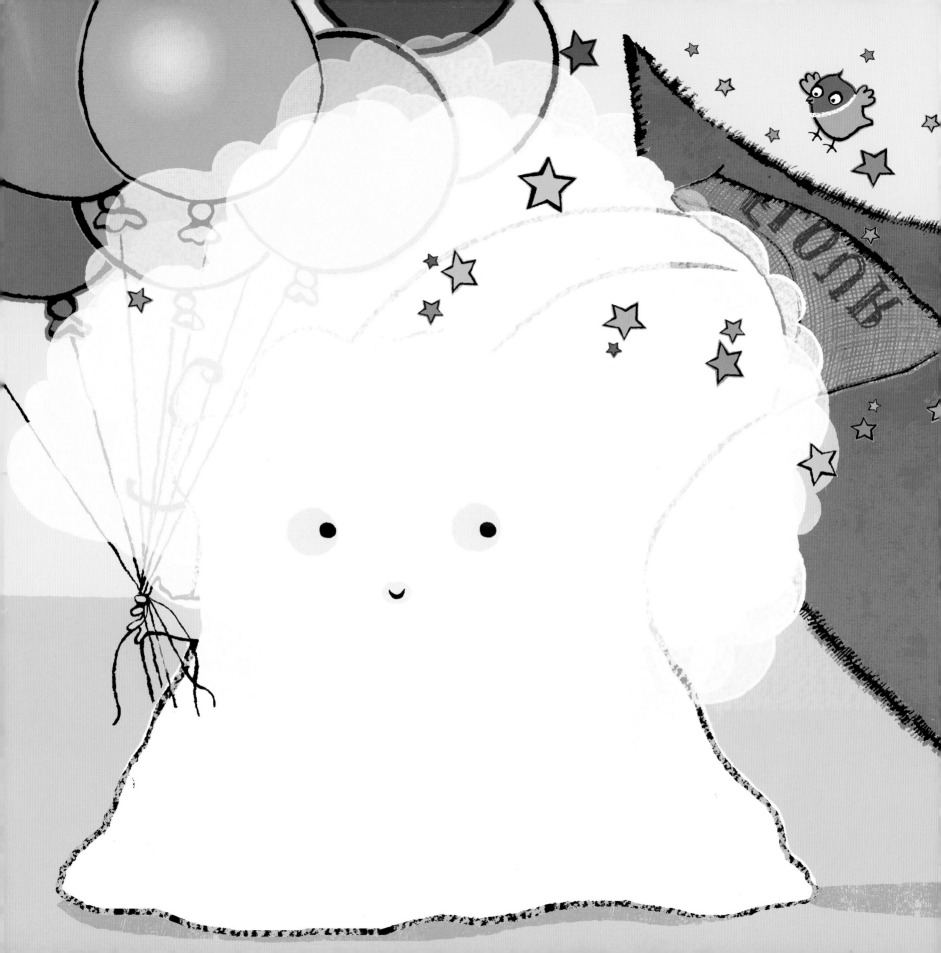

Emily giggled. "Not this kind of **flour,** Foxy!
The kind that grows in the ground!"

Even Foxy laughed. "Whoops!"
A swish of his tail, and the floor was
a garden of beautiful flowers.

"Ooh . . . I love rainbows," said Emily.
"Anything else?" asked Foxy, still hopeful.

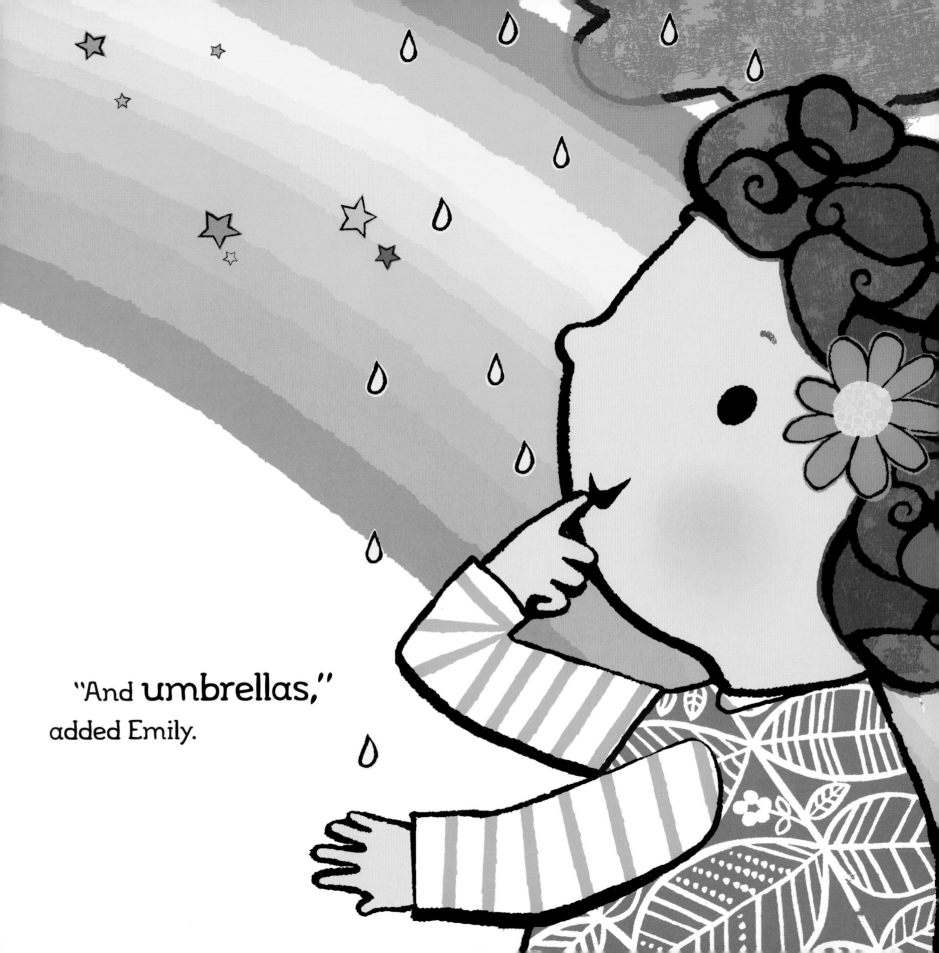

"And **umbrellas**," added Emily.

"I know I will need a lot of **hearts!**" Emily said.

"No, not **larks**!
Not **tarts**!"

"That's better!"

Foxy loved all the hearts, but something was still missing. "Emily, I think you forgot something important," said Foxy.

"But Foxy, I don't have room
to draw anything else on this
Valentine's Day card."

"Valentine's Day is not about *what* you love,"
Foxy explained. "It's about *who* you love."